Wendi Schuller is a published author, hypnotherapist, and practitioner of Neuro-Linguistic Programming (NLP). Her previous book is *The Global Guide to Divorce*. She has been a nurse in elementary schools. She has traveled to over sixty countries, including jungles on three continents. Ms. Schuller volunteers weekly at a cat rescue charity.

Jack Jack
THE JUNGLE CAT

Written by Wendi Schuller

Illustrated by Joe Lundy

AUSTIN MACAULEY PUBLISHERS™

LONDON * CAMBRIDGE * NEW YORK * SHARJAH

Copyright © Wendi Schuller (2019)

Ordering Information:

Quantity sales: special discounts are available on quantity purchases by corporations, associations, and others. For details, contact the publisher at the address below.

Schuller, Wendi
Jack Jack the Jungle Cat

ISBN 9781641824132 (Paperback)
ISBN 9781641824149 (Hardback)
ISBN 9781641824156 (E-Book)

The main category of the book — JUVENILE FICTION / Animals / Lions, Tigers, Leopards, etc.

www.austinmacauley.com/us

First Published (2019)
Austin Macauley Publishers LLC
40 Wall Street, 28th Floor
New York, NY 10005
USA

mail-usa@austinmacauley.com
+1 (646) 5125767

The King of the Jungle is Jack Jack the Cat. He climbs the tree to visit Iggy the bat.

Jungle sounds are everywhere. Is that a parrot in the air?

Hear the drums? Listen to the beat. Jack Jack are those friendly feet?

Are you chasing a slithering snake – for fun?
It is a deadly King Cobra – Jack Jack run!

Look up into the tops of trees. Is that a monkey on a trapeze?

These friends share many adventures together.
Take cover – here comes stormy weather.

Puddles appear after heavy rain showers.
See Herbie the frog among the lily flowers?

Elephants are splashing in the river with Jack Jack's buddy.
Rolling around when playing games, gets the wee ones muddy.

"Oh, monkey do you think the crocodile wants to play?"
Jack Jack he is a dangerous creature – stay away!

Birds gather around the two and sing in chorus.
"Monkey do you think this concert is just for us?"

The two search for their elephant pals with painted faces.
Their parade is to the temple and surrounding places.

It is a celebration with food, music, and dance.
"Think we can sneak in? Let us take a chance."

Jungle games are about to begin. Get to the starting line
– who will win?

At the birthday party each one puts on their hat.
Someone is missing. Where is Jack Jack the cat?

Can you find Jack Jack the cat?

Through the dense rainforest he hears his mother's call.
"Jack Jack come eat. It is dinnertime for all."

Jungle Animals

The most common species of monkeys in Southeast Asia is the macaque. These are the impish ones that hang around the temples trying to beg or steal some food. They are cute, but can be a bit aggressive. They have a light brownish color and are one and a half to two feet tall. Macaques are very social and live in groups.

Tigers are the largest cats and are endangered. These solitary creatures live in Asia and in Siberia. India has the largest number of tigers of any country. They have become extinct in Cambodia: mainly due to poaching and deforestation. The Cambodian government is planning on reintroducing them in the wild with the assistance of wildlife and conservation charities. There are more tigers in captivity than in the wild.

Leopards are also solitary creatures and are great swimmers. They are nocturnal and are more active at night. They can be spotted, black or the white snow leopard to blend in with their environment. They spend much of their time in the trees. Leopards are the smallest of the biggest of the four cats (tigers, lions, jaguars, and leopards).

Asian elephants are smaller than the African ones, with smaller ears and pink spots on trunks, ears or faces. They are social and live in groups headed by the matriarch (oldest female). They spend a large part of their day eating grass, leaves and bark. Elephants live near water to drink, cool off and splash around in it. Venomous snakes in Southeast Asia include cobras, vipers, keel backs and kraits. The jungle has parrots and other colorful birds.

Author's Note

Jack Jack the Jungle Cat is based upon a real cat who is my frequent house guest. He climbs up the cat pillar as if it were a tree. He looks as if he were having an imaginary adventure. Jack Jack is pulled out of his jungle world when I call him for mealtime to eat with my three cats. He loves his stuffed toy as Jack Jack in the story enjoys his monkey friend.

CPSIA information can be obtained
at www.ICGtesting.com
Printed in the USA
BVHW011156020519
547203BV00002B/28/P